Home for Meow

Show and Tail

D0088562

Home for Meow

Show and Tail

Reese Eschmann

Scholastic Inc.

Copyright © 2022 by Charisse Eschmann

All rights reserved. Published by Scholastic Inc., *Publishers since 1920*. SCHOLASTIC and associated logos are trademarks and/or registered trademarks of Scholastic Inc.

The publisher does not have any control over and does not assume any responsibility for author or third-party websites or their content.

Library of Congress Cataloging-in-Publication Data available

ISBN 978-1-338-78399-5

10 9 8 7 6 5 4 3 2 1   22 23 24 25 26

Printed in the U.S.A.   40

First edition, July 2022

Book design by Stephanie Yang

Interior art © 2022 by Wendy Tan

Table of Contents

1

Bubbles's Bulging Belly

Bubbles's belly is huge! She waddles around the
kiddie pool Mama filled with blankets for her.
The pool is in the corner of our living room, right
below the window that gets the best morning
light.

"Kira, how many kittens do you think Bubbles

is going to have?" asks my little brother, Ryan. We're kneeling by the side of the kiddie pool. "I bet she'll have at least eighteen."

"Eighteen?" Mama says. She stands over us. "Let's hope she only has one or two. We don't have much room for new cats right now."

"I think she'll have six perfectly perfect kittens," I say. "Because she has six stripes across her belly."

Bubbles is a brown-and-black-striped tabby cat. Earlier this month, the animal shelter brought her to stay at our family's cat café, The Purrfect Cup. I named her Bubbles because her belly keeps getting rounder and bigger, like when I blow air into my gum to make a big bubble. And Mama keeps saying she looks like she's about to pop.

Bubbles paws at the blankets in the kiddie pool and meows loudly. Mama says she's nesting. That means she's going to have her kittens really soon, so she's making everything warm and safe for them. Bubbles pulls the blankets around with her teeth, arranging them into a cozy nest for her babies to sleep in. Dad says that when Mama was pregnant with me, she was nesting too. She filled the freezer with trays of macaroni and cheese, and she sewed extra cushions for her rocking chair.

"Do you think Bubbles will have her babies today?" I ask Mama.

Mama smiles. "I think that's a real possibility. I'm going to bring her to Dr. Delgado this morning."

I frown. "Why does she have to go to the animal hospital? Can't she have her kittens here?"

"Don't worry, Kira," says Mama. "Dr. Delgado is the best vet around. Bubbles will be in good hands. And I'll bring the kiddie pool to make sure she's comfortable."

Dad opens the door to our apartment. He's been baking in the café kitchen all morning. I can tell because he's got flour on his forehead.

"Kira, Ryan, ready for school?" he asks.

"Yup," says Ryan. He leans down and pets

Bubbles very gently. "You're a strong and fierce woman, Bubbles. You've totally got this."

I cross my arms. I, Kira Parker, have a lot of *great ideas*, and going to school while Bubbles is having her kittens is not one of them. I remember how worried I was when Mama went to the hospital to have Ryan.

"I think I'll go to the hospital with Bubbles," I say.

Dad crosses his arms back at me. "You can't miss the first day of school to watch a cat have kittens, Kira."

"You'll feel much better when you're distracted with your friends," says Mama. "Everything will be okay. The hospital is the best place to have a baby—or a kitten. Don't you remember when I went to the hospital when I was pregnant?"

"I do. That's why I'm so worried! You came back with *Ryan*. Are you sure that was a good idea?"

Ryan sticks his tongue out at me. "I'm the best thing that ever happened to this family."

Mama pulls us in for a hug and squishes our faces into her arms. "You're *both* the best things that ever happened to me. And Bubbles is going to be so happy to meet her kittens."

I sigh. "Can I name them when I get home? I have a lot of good ideas for kitten names."

"Of course," says Mama. "You and Ryan can both name them."

I kiss my fingers, then touch them to Bubbles's

head. "Good luck," I whisper. "I'll be back soon."

Bubbles looks up at me with her big, gold eyes. She blinks four times, then leans forward so I can scratch her ears. I imagine that each blink is a word and she's saying, "I can do this." I think Ryan was right. Bubbles *is* a strong and fierce woman.

I grab my backpack and follow Dad downstairs into the café. We're opening late today because Dad wants to walk us to school, so there aren't any customers in The Purrfect Cup. But even without customers, The Purrfect Cup is packed!

Mama was right when she said we didn't have much room for kittens. There are cats every-where. They're sleeping on top of shelves, sitting in the customers' chairs, and cuddling in the corners. When I look at them, I feel like a chocolate chip melting into cookie dough—warm and surrounded by sweetness. These cats are my best friends.

Our family's cat and my *very best* friend, Pepper, leaps down from one of the shelves. I catch her in my arms.

"I missed you, Pepper," I say, snuggling into her fur. "I know you're suspicious of Bubbles's belly. But I told you, there are no aliens in there. Just kittens."

Pepper wriggles free of my hug and jumps on the ground. She's been sleeping in the café ever since Bubbles started nesting. Even though

Pepper loves hanging out down here with all the cats, she likes having the apartment to herself. I think she and Dad would both agree we don't need more cats—or cat hair—on our sofa. But if there isn't room for the kittens in the café or up in our apartment, where will they go?

"Dad, where are the kittens going to live?" I ask.

"Not here," Dad says quickly. *Too quickly.* I frown. He clears his throat. "I mean, I'm so excited for the miracle of life and all that...the kittens will probably stay with us until they're old enough to be adopted. Mama and I are hoping it won't take long to find them homes."

"I hope it takes years!" says Ryan. "Can you

imagine if we had eighteen kittens? I could train a whole cat army and we could drive around in a Jeep and—"

Ryan spends the whole walk to school talking about all the things he'd do with a cat army, like steal a spaceship and eat all the cheese on the moon. I'm still thinking about how many kittens it would take to steal a spaceship when school starts. My teacher, Ms. Pettina, puts the first math worksheet of the year down on my desk. I groan. Math makes less sense than a cat army going to the moon. I try to reword the math problem in terms I know.

Leo has 33 ~~pieces of candy~~ cats left over from Halloween. If he gives 14 ~~pieces~~ cats to Mark and

11 ~~pieces~~ cats to Anna, how many ~~pieces~~ cats does he have left?

I sigh. Changing candy to cats doesn't make solving the problem any easier. My brain feels like egg whites that have been whipped for too long. At least Ms. Pettina let me sit next to my best human friend, Alex. She's wearing new pink cat-eye glasses and a matching pink sweatshirt.

"Nice first-day outfit," I whisper, leaning toward her desk.

"Thanks. I thought you were going to wear your lucky sweatshirt?" she whispers back.

I look down and realize I'm still wearing my paw-print pajama shirt and pants. My granny bought them for me—the shirt even has my name

sewn above the pocket! But pajamas are for sleeping, not math. I got distracted by Bubbles's bulging belly and didn't finish getting ready for school!

I forget to whisper. "Alex! Oh no, I'm wearing pajamas!"

Alex nods seriously. "I know—"

Ms. Pettina clears her throat. "Kira and Alex, do you have something to share?"

Alex gulps. Everyone is looking at us. I need to distract them from my pajamas! I blurt out, "My cat is about to pop! She's full of kittens!"

Ms. Pettina raises her eyebrows. *Ugh.* My cheeks feel warm. I squish them between my hands. I feel like a piece of bread heating up in an embarrassment toaster. I'm not sure why I thought talking about kittens would be better than admitting my mistake. Everyone can see my pajamas anyway.

"Um, thank you for sharing, Kira," says Ms.

Pettina. "I hope everything goes well with your cat and her kittens."

Ms. Pettina smiles. I can't believe she isn't mad. Turns out talking about Bubbles popping wasn't my worst idea ever.

"That's actually a good introduction to our class project for this quarter," Ms. Pettina says. "We're going to have a pet-themed show and tell at the end of November, right before our Thanksgiving break."

I sit up straight in my seat. *Pet-themed show and tell?* Now *this* is my jam. And not just any jam. It's Dad's homemade strawberry jam smeared on a freshly baked biscuit. I get to do a whole project about my cats! Pepper is going to be so excited to meet all my classmates.

A bunch of kids' hands fly into the air.

Ms. Pettina points at a girl sitting in the front row. "Yes?"

"Hello, Ms. Pettina, you might not recognize me because I didn't go to school in this building last year. My name is Sara."

Ms. Pettina raises her eyebrows again. "Sara, yes, I met your parents at orientation. Do you have a question?"

Sara nods. "What do we do for show and tell if we don't have a pet?"

"Don't worry, I have a few options for students who don't have pets. You can write about your favorite animal from a book you've read, or make a presentation on scientific facts about pets."

The rest of the students put their hands down. Ms. Pettina looks around the classroom. "Hmm, did you all have the same question?"

A bunch of my classmates nod. That means they don't have pets, either.

My brain works so fast, I can almost hear it whirring like a blender. Bubbles's kittens are going to need homes. And these kids need pets. I may not be good at solving math problems, but I can already picture my classmates showing their newly adopted kittens to the class. I smile. This is a *great idea*.

Maybe pajamas are my new lucky sweatshirt.

2

Perfectly Perfect

Mr. Anderson meets Ryan and me after school.

He runs the best art shop in town, Anderson's

Artsy Abode. He's one of our favorite customers!

Mama sends him lots of free treats from the café,

and he lets me try out new art supplies before he

sells them.

"Hey, Mr. Anderson," I say. "What are you doing here? Are you donating more markers to the school?"

"Or are you trying to learn math?" Ryan asks. "Let me tell you, don't bother. First grade is hard. You should probably just use your phone if you want to add stuff up."

Mr. Anderson chuckles. "No, no, I hope I've learned enough math. And that's a good idea, Kira, I think I do have some markers in the back of the shop. I'd love to donate them. But I'm here because your parents asked me to pick you up! Your mom is at the animal hospital and your dad is running the café."

Sometimes Mama and Dad ask Mr. Anderson

to pick us up from school when they're busy. But I didn't know Mama would be with Dr. Delgado all day.

"Mama is still at the hospital?" Ryan asks.

"That must mean Bubbles is really having her babies today!" I squeal. I feel more excited than I did when Pepper and I had the *great idea* to make fish-flavored cat ice cream. "So you're taking us to the animal hospital to see them?"

"Hmm...I don't know." Mr. Anderson scratches the white hairs on his chin. "Are you supposed to go to the animal hospital?"

"Yes!" Ryan and I say at the same time. Ryan looks up at Mr. Anderson. I don't usually describe my little brother as *cute*, but sometimes he makes his eyes wide and sweet and grown-ups do anything he asks. It's like he's putting extra frosting on a cupcake and waving it in front of Mr. Anderson's face.

"Aww, you really want to see the kittens, don't you? All right, then," says Mr. Anderson. "To Dr. Delgado we go!"

I squeeze Ryan into a hug. "Aargh, get off me!" he grumbles. The cuteness melts away from his face and he becomes my annoying, hug-hating brother again.

"Nice work, Ryan," I say. "I can't wait to meet Bubbles's babies. I hope they're okay."

"I don't even care about the kittens," Ryan

whispers. "I just don't want to have to do any chores at the café."

I roll my eyes. He totally cares about the kittens.

Dr. Delgado's Animal Hospital is at the edge of town. It sits right in front of the big road that we use to go to the city to visit our granny. The hospital is a plain brick building. It looks so boring compared to The Purrfect Cup and the other shops on our street—it doesn't even have a colorful sign out front! Inside, all the walls are white. It's too clean. Where are all the cozy cat beds? No wonder Pepper doesn't like going to the vet.

The lady at the desk is talking to a man about

his sick turtle. When she sees us, she points down the hall.

"Third door on the left!"

I suck in a big breath. I feel like I did that time I spilled a batch of Dad's homemade caramel on the floor and it got all over my shoes. *Sticky.* I'm stuck to the clean white floors and don't think I can move.

"Mr. Anderson," I say. My voice sounds squeaky. "Do you think the kittens are okay? Mama was so tired when she got back from the hospital when Ryan was born. Do you think Bubbles is sleepy too?"

"I'm sure everything is going well," Mr. Anderson says kindly. "How about you wait here, and I'll make sure that they're ready for you and Ryan?"

My heart pounds with every step Mr. Anderson takes down the hallway. Ryan's fingers grab hold of my hand and he squeezes hard.

I try to make my voice less squeaky. "When you and your cat army go to space, will you name a star after me?"

Ryan nods. I hug him again, and this time he hugs back.

Down the hall, the third door on the left opens. It's Mama! She smiles and waves at us to join her. My feet unstick and I run down the hallway.

"Kira, slow down!" Mama warns, but I'm too excited to stop. I push through the door.

Bubbles is lying down in her kiddie pool, and next to her are the tiniest, cutest, fuzziest kittens I've ever seen! Their little bodies wiggle around, and they flop over one another to get closer to their mama. Bubbles watches them patiently. She licks the head of one of her babies. It yawns. Its teeny-tiny mouth opens up wide, and it sticks out its pink tongue. I start laughing out loud. I can't help myself. It feels like my heart is about to explode! I count the kittens.

"One-two-three-four-five-six! I was right! I knew Bubbles would have six perfect kittens." I turn to Ryan. "Sorry, I don't think that's enough for your cat army."

But Ryan isn't listening. His hands are covering his mouth and he's jumping up and down in excitement.

"Hi, Kira and Ryan," says Dr. Delgado. "I'm happy to report that Bubbles did fantastic! She and the kittens are very healthy and happy. Would you like to hold one?"

"Would I like to hold one?" I squeal. "Are cookies sweet? Do cats love naps?"

Dr. Delgado laughs and puts up his hand. "Okay, okay, I get it," he says. "Of course you want to hold one. First you need to wash your hands and put on a pair of gloves."

When Ryan and I are ready, we sit beside the kiddie pool. Bubbles had two kittens with

brown-and-black stripes, two kittens with gray stripes, one orange kitten, and one black kitten.

Dr. Delgado carefully picks up the orange kitten and places it in my outstretched hands.

"This one is a girl," he says.

She fits perfectly in my palm. Her orange fur

stands up on end and her eyes are closed and her nose is the pinkest pink. I want to giggle and cry and sing and hold her for every second until the end of time. But as much as I want to keep her *fur-ever*, I know that won't be possible. My heart aches. I think about my *great idea* and it makes me feel a little better. My classmates are going to be so excited to bring these kittens home!

Dr. Delgado hands Ryan a striped kitten. "A boy," he says.

Ryan holds the kitten close to his chest. He tucks in his chin so his nose is almost rubbing against the kitten's soft fur.

"I love you," he whispers. "You're my favorite."

Bubbles sits up and watches us holding her kittens. I hold out my hands and she leans forward to lick the orange kitten.

"Good job, Bubbles," I say. "You're a great mama."

The orange kitten opens her tiny mouth and yawns. She stretches her sweet little paws and wiggles around in my hand.

Dr. Delgado hands Mama a scale. "As I was saying, you can use this to weigh the kittens to track their growth. But Bubbles's natural instincts should do most of the work! Call me with any questions. I'll see you soon."

"Thanks for everything," Mama says. "This has been an exhausting but rewarding day. We're excited to watch the kittens grow. How long should we wait before we start looking for adoptive homes?"

"The kittens can go to their adoptive homes when they are twelve weeks old. But you can start looking earlier than that! People love newborn kittens," Dr. Delgado responds.

"Mama, when is twelve weeks from now?" I ask.

She does some quick math in her head. "Um, mid-November?" she says.

Ms. Pettina said the show and tell would be at the end of November, right before Thanksgiving. That's perfect! The kittens will have time to go to their new homes before the show and tell. I smile.

Mama looks down at me and the orange kitten. "You look pretty cozy with that cutie, Kira. What's on your mind? You said you had some good ideas for names."

"Actually," I say. "I got an *even better* idea today at school."

Mama laughs. "Of course you did."

3

The List of Pawsibilities

"I didn't realize there was so much to learn about kittens," I say. It's been one week since they were born, and I'm learning something new every day! Like I didn't know that kittens don't open their eyes right away. Ryan and I have been watching as each tiny kitten slowly learns to open its eyes.

"C'mon, Meatloaf, you can do it." Ryan leans in close to the black kitten. He's the smallest and sleepiest of the litter, and the only kitten who hasn't opened his eyes yet. "You're my favorite. Don't you want to see my beautiful face?"

"Ugh, please stop calling him Meatloaf," I say. Ryan named all the cats after his least favorite foods. Broccoli, Peas, Beans, and Tuna are the striped kittens. Ryan calls the orange kitten Hot Sauce and the black kitten Meatloaf.

I pick up the black kitten. "He's too cute for a name like *Meatloaf*. I bet he won't open his eyes until you stop embarrassing him. And you know Mama agreed we should let the families who adopt the kittens name them."

"Well, we have to call them something. And I haven't heard much about these families."

I scowl. "That's only because I'm still research-ing my plan!" I set Meatloaf down and pick up one of the striped kittens, Beans. His eyes are so big they take up most of his face. He looks at me so seriously. I hope he isn't worried about being adopted. "Don't listen to him, Beans. My great idea is going *great*. I'm going to find you an awesome family that will love you so much! Promise."

I press my finger against Beans's tiny paw. His itty-bitty nails are soft against my skin. I can't believe that one day he'll grow to have full claws like Pepper! Yesterday when I tried to bring

Pepper upstairs to look at the kittens, she used her claws to climb up super high on one of the cat trees in the café. I couldn't reach her even when I climbed onto a chair!

"Kira," Mama's voice calls up to us from downstairs in the café. "Alex is here."

"See?" I say to Beans, but mostly to Ryan. "Backup has arrived! Everything is going according to plan."

I set Beans back in the kiddie pool and run downstairs. Alex is waiting for me at one of the tables in the café. Pepper is sitting on her lap. Alex's mom, Mrs. Patel, stands in the doorway of the café and waves at me.

"Alex got a whole bunch of materials at

Mr. Anderson's," says Mrs. Patel. "You two must be up to something!"

"Aren't they always?" Mama laughs from behind the café counter. "Do you want to come in for a bit?"

"Oh, no thank you," says Mrs. Patel. "My allergies are extra awful today. In fact, I think some of the cat hair is floating this way."

Mrs. Patel swats the air in front of her. Then she lets out the loudest sneeze I've ever heard. "I'd better go," she sniffs. "Have fun, Alex! Don't bring any cat hair home."

Alex sighs as I sit down next to her. "I wish my mom liked animals."

"She *is* right about cat hair," I say. "It sticks to

everything. You already have Pepper's hair all over your shirt!"

I reach out for Pepper, but she scowls at me and leaps away. Alex looks worried.

"Why did Pepper run away from you? She never does that!"

I shrug. "Pepper is mad that the kittens are living in the apartment. She likes having the upstairs space all to herself!"

"I'm sorry, Kira," Alex says. "That must be hard."

"Yeah, those poor kittens! It's not their fault they keep growing and taking up more space!"

Alex looks confused. "I was actually saying it must be hard for Pepper—"

"Let's not talk about Pepper anymore," I say. I don't even see where she went. She must be hiding. "We should make our list!"

"Good idea," Alex says. "What supplies did you find upstairs?"

"I got paper, markers, and some glitter pens, just in case!" I pull the materials out of a paper bag.

"Perfect!" Alex says. "I overheard Devin and Jorge talking about the show and tell yesterday. I think we've spied on everyone in the class now! We just need to get our research organized."

All week, Alex and I have been trying to find out which of our classmates don't have pets. We've been doing a lot of snooping around at lunch and recess, paying attention to which kids have dog hair on their lunch boxes and listening to people talk about show and tell. I scribbled all my research on a napkin, which was a bad idea because I forgot and used the napkin to clean up spilled milk this morning. That's why we need to put our notes somewhere more official.

Alex lays a big piece of poster paper on the table. I write in bubble letters at the top, then Alex colors in my bubble letters while I write our classmates' names.

The List of Pawsibilities

Alex

Sophia

Freddy

Martrell

Jorge

Sara

Devin

Ellie

Aaliyah

"There are nine kids who don't have pets," I say. "And we only need to find adoptive homes for six cats. This is going to be easy!"

Alex nods. "I think you're right. I mean, who can resist kittens?"

"Well, I can think of one person," I say. I pick up a purple marker and cross Alex's name off the list.

Alex—mom is allergic to cats

Alex sighs. "I wish I could have a pet."

"I wish you could too. But at least you have me and all the cats in the café! And you can come here anytime you want," I say.

"Thanks, Kira," Alex says. "You're a good friend."

"Kira, look at this!" Mama calls out. I turn around to see her holding her phone. She's taking a picture of Pepper, who's sitting on a shelf on the other side of the café. "Look at Pepper's face. She looks like those Grumpy Cat memes, doesn't she? I'm going to put this on the café's website."

Pepper does look grumpy. Like, *super* grumpy. Her usually cute face is all mushed up like a muffin that's been stepped on. And she's glaring right at me!

"I didn't even know Pepper's face could do that," Alex whispers. She looks scared.

"Pepper, what's your problem?" I ask. I stand up and cross the café, reaching out my arms to pick her up. But when I get close, she leaps from the shelf to the top of a cat tree. I chase after her, but she jumps from tree to chair to table—all over the café! It's like that time I tried to teach Pepper how to do tricks for a dog show and she wouldn't listen!

Pepper knocks a customer's teacup over in her hurry to get away from me. The tea gets all over her fur—and the customer's lap! Then she jumps onto our table and walks over our poster with her wet paws, before settling in Alex's lap.

"Oh no," I say to the customer. "I'm so sorry! Pepper never acts like this!"

Mama hands me a towel and offers to give the customer a fresh cup of tea and a free cookie. Alex holds on to Pepper tightly.

"That was so odd," Mama says after I finish cleaning up. "Kira and Alex, why don't you take Pepper over to Mr. Anderson's for a bit? Maybe she needs some fresh air."

"I think what Pepper needs is some time to think about why she's being such a grumpy-face." I grab the tea-stained poster and ignore the prickly feeling in my chest. Pepper is my best friend. This isn't how best friends are supposed to act. I take a deep breath and remind myself that there are six perfect kittens upstairs who need my help.

"Besides," I say, "I've got more important work to do."

4

Maybes and Monster Cookies

I sit down next to the fifth kid on my List of

Pawsibilities. Alex has a cold and stayed home

from school today. That means I have to talk to

all the *pawsible families* for the kittens by myself.

But Dad always says that we should be "up for a

challenge." I'm pretty sure I am because I was so

nervous that I stayed up late and woke up early. That's a lot of being up for stuff. Three more kids on my list already said no, but I have high hopes for Pawsible Family Number Five.

"Hey, Jorge," I say.

"Hello, Kira Parker," he says, looking at me seriously. "What are you up to these days? We haven't spoken since kindergarten."

Kindergarten to third grade is a lot of time to cover. I'm not sure what to say. "Um, I'm up to the same stuff as always, I guess. Sorry we haven't talked since kindergarten."

"That's all right. Your main interest is cats and mine is engineering. We don't have much in common. What'd you come over to talk about?" He raises a hopeful eyebrow and smiles. "How planes are made?"

"Uh . . . I wanted to talk about cats." I see his smile start to drop. "I mean, kittens! Kittens are so cute, right?"

Jorge shrugs. "I do know a few things about kittens. I read an article that said baby kittens don't know how to go to the bathroom on their own, so their moms massage their bellies until it happens. Did you know that?"

I make a grumpy face that probably looks like Pepper's. "Yeah, I learned that last week," I say. "But I've been trying to forget."

This isn't going well, so I pull out my secret weapon: cookies! I made them last night using

cat-shaped cookie cutters, but something went wrong and my dough spread in the oven. The cookies look more like blobs with whiskers than kittens, but they're still delicious.

"Do you want a cookie?" I ask Jorge.

"Wow, monster cookies! Cool!" He takes one and stuffs it in his mouth. While he's chewing, I give him my pitch. Mama and Dad told me about two different kinds of pitches: the business kind, where you convince someone that your idea is good, and the baseball kind, where you throw a ball at them. I'm using the first kind of pitch. I clear my throat.

"So, Jorge, I noticed that you don't have a pet for show and tell, and I might have a solution to your problem! A cat at our café had six perfect kittens, and they're going to be available for adoption in time for show and tell! Kittens love engineers. I bet you could build some really cool shelves for your kitten to climb!"

I wish I had a third arm so I could pat myself on the back. That part about engineering was pretty good! I didn't even know I was going to say that until the words spilled out my mouth. It's like that time I spilled almond extract into my muffin batter and accidentally made the best lemon muffins *ever*.

Jorge swallows his cookie. "I do like building shelves. But I also read that researchers tried to study cats, and they gave up because cats never do what you expect them to do."

I wish Jorge didn't read so much. I try to come up with a new pitch. "That's what makes cats so awesome! They're silly and stubborn and it's funny to watch them. They're not like dogs that jump on you and give you slobbery kisses and stuff. You have to *earn* a cat's love, and that makes it extra special. I bet those researchers didn't do anything to make the cats love them."

Jorge looks thoughtful. "You know, Kira, you've convinced me."

"I *have*?"

"Yes, I'm going to get a puppy. I love slobbery kisses. And I can build something cool for it, just like you said. That was a good idea. Maybe I'll build a doghouse! Can I have another cookie?"

I make a face at him. I don't know why my pitch didn't work. Maybe I should have tried the baseball kind. "You can have half a cookie," I grumble.

"Sweet, thanks!" he says. He stuffs his face

with half a cookie and leaves. *Uh-oh.* I'm running out of pawsibilities. I get a tight feeling in my stomach, like maybe that third arm I wanted to pat myself on the back with is now squeezing my insides. What will happen to the kittens if I can't find homes for them? I cross Jorge's name off my list.

The List of Pawsibilities

~~Alex~~—mom is allergic to cats

~~Sophia~~—saving up to buy either a monkey or a bearded dragon

~~Freddy~~—thinks litter boxes are gross

~~Martrell~~—terrified of whiskers

~~Jorge~~—getting a puppy

Sara

Devin

Ellie

Aaliyah

Just then, the new girl, Sara, slides onto the bench next to me. "Hi," she says. "Is that my name on your poster?"

"Um, yeah," I say. "But I'm not a spy. I'm Kira."

"Yeah, you're not very sneaky. Nice to meet you, Kira," Sara says. She reads my poster. "'The List of *Paw*-sibilities.' That's funny. Does this have to do with those paw-print pajamas you wore on the first day of school? Or wait, am *I* a possibility?"

She looks hopeful. The tightness in my stomach goes away. Time to forget about Jorge's slobbery puppy and focus on my next pawsible kitten family!

"You're new in town, right?" I ask. "My family owns the best cat café in Bloomington, The Purrfect Cup. You should come by sometime."

"How many cat cafés are there in this town?"

"Only one! But we'd be the best even if there were a hundred."

"Cool. I'd love to see it," Sara says, smiling. "I like making lists too. Want to see mine?"

She opens her bag and takes out the biggest book I've ever seen. The title on the cover says *The Iliad*. I don't remember our teacher asking us to read that. Sara opens the book and a piece of green paper falls out. She shows it to me.

Things to Do in Third Grade

1. Have a sleepover.

2. Take Mama J to the corn maze.

3. Learn how to bake a cake.

4. Make three new friends.

5. Get Mama P and Daddy F the best Halloween present
EVER.

6. Find out why ancient Romans didn't use soap.

"You have a Mama J and a Mama P?" I ask.
"That's cool. I only have a Mama . . . Mama."

"Yeah, Mama J is my birth mama and Mama P
is my adoptive mom. They both have pajama
shirts with their names on them, like your paw-
print shirt! I wish I had one."

"I can ask my granny where she got it," I offer.

"Also, I didn't know people gave their parents Halloween presents. Am I supposed to do that? I usually eat all my candy . . ."

Sara laughs. "I don't share my candy, either. But Halloween is my parents' favorite holiday. So I get them a present."

My brain runs as fast as a cat chasing a mouse-shaped toy. In movies and stuff, parents always buy pets for their kids as presents. But maybe it could work the other way around . . .

"I heard you talking to Jorge about adopting cats," Sara says. "Do you know anything about Odysseus? He was this Greek dude who was trying to get back to his home for twenty years. Maybe having a cat is like that."

I think hard for a second, trying to figure out what she means. Then I say the smartest thing I can think of. "Huh?"

"Because you said you have to *earn* their love. It takes a long time. But in the end, it's worth it, right?"

Finally, someone who *gets* cats. Some people just don't understand.

"Exactly!" I say. "It's totally worth it. When a cat comes up to you and wants to snuggle, it's worth more than all the treasure in the world. It's like . . . the best present EVER!"

I look at her hopefully, but she's looking down at my list. I might have to try a little harder if I want her to give a kitten to her parents for Halloween.

"Hey," Sara says, reading the rest of my list of names. "Devin lives in my building. What if I help you with your list, and you help me with mine?"

I smile. "That's a *great idea*."

Sara asks to borrow my pen, then she makes a small change to her list.

4. Make ~~three~~ two new friends.

♥ 🐾 ♥

Sara introduces me to Devin during recess. We stand off to the side while the other kids run around and practice Hula-Hooping. I give Devin a cookie and ask if he likes kittens.

"KITTENS! I LOVE kittens," he shouts. "We have three cats at my house."

"Wait, you already have a pet?" I ask. "Didn't you raise your hand to ask about the pet show and tell? And Alex heard you talking to Jorge about not knowing what to do on show and tell day."

"MAN, these cookies are good," Devin says, stuffing a whiskered blob into his mouth. "I was raising my hand to go to the bathroom. And I was telling Jorge I didn't know which cat I should bring. Do you think Ms. Pettina would let me show all three?"

I sigh. Too many cats is a good problem to have. But I need more pawsible families to become real adoptive families! Sara is my only "maybe" so far, and she didn't actually say maybe. She just said something about Greek dudes.

"We were going to ask if you wanted to adopt a kitten from my family's cat café."

"The Purrfect Cup? That place is AWESOME! My mom got two of our cats there." Devin scratches his chin. I wonder if he thinks *he's* got whiskers. He doesn't. I don't think boys grow whiskers until they're, like, thirteen or something. "Hmm, I already have one gray cat, one black cat, and one white cat. What colors do you have?"

He leans in close and whispers, "Purple? I'd

pay a lot of money for a purple cat. Especially if it had green eyes."

Sara whispers back. "I didn't know purple cats existed. Were they made by the goddess Bastet?"

"I don't know who that is, but that sounds RIGHT," Devin says. He's shouting again. "Kira, do you know this goddess?"

"No, but the kittens' mama, Bubbles, is basically a goddess," I say. "She had six kittens in one day. Some of them are striped and one of them is orange—"

"ORANGE?" Devin stuffs two more cookies in his mouth. "Okay, okay, this is interesting. I gotta ask my mom about this."

He turns and runs toward the door to get back into the building. I don't know where he's going. It's still recess! But I think Devin might be another "maybe."

"That was exciting!" Sara says. "Devin is kinda funny, right? Do you think that counts as making a new friend?"

"I'm not sure," I say. "I'm going to put him down as a maybe!"

"Okay, me too," Sara says. "Let's talk to the last two kids on your list!"

We find Ellie and Aaliyah drawing with chalk in the corner of the playground. I love drawing! Mr. Anderson always lets me draw when I visit his shop. But he doesn't have any chalk. Next time I see him, I'll tell him he should buy some. That'll be a *great idea* for him!

"Hey, Aaliyah," I say. "Can we borrow some chalk?"

"Sure!" she says. Maybe my drawing can be my pitch. I use the chalk to draw six kittens on the ground. I use yellow chalk to draw their big eyes and pink chalk for their little toes. I draw a few extra whiskers on each kitten because drawing whiskers is easy. My drawings aren't as cute as the real thing, but the chalk kittens look much better than the cookie blobs.

"Ooh, that's cute!" Aaliyah says. "I like the colors."

Aaliyah's outfit is bright and bold. She has on

lots of bracelets and her shoes are sparkling clean. I bet she'd love a cute kitten like Broccoli. Broccoli loves hiding in piles of clothes, and she always licks her fur until it's sparkling clean!

"These are the kittens that live at my family's cat café," I say. "They're WAY cuter in person. You and Ellie don't have pets, right? You could adopt a kitten, if you want!"

"Oh yeah, your cat café is called The Purrfect Cup!" Ellie says. "My mom owns the fish store on Main Street, Something Fishy. I think our moms go to business meetings together sometimes."

"You have a fish store but no pet fish?" Sara asks.

"My mom says she spends all day cleaning out

fish tanks. She doesn't want to do it again when she gets home!"

"Cats and fish are very different," I say. I'm pretty sure that's true. "Most of my cats don't even like water! Maybe your mom would like a change of face."

"Don't you mean, a change of *pace*?" Aaliyah asks.

"I thought it was change of face," I say. "Because kittens and fish have different faces. What does change of *pace* mean?"

Aaliyah shrugs. Ellie looks thoughtful.

"My mom might agree to getting a kitten. But I'm not sure." She shudders. "Cats creep me out a little bit. They're always staring at you."

"And they have claws, don't they?" Aaliyah says. "They can scratch you!"

Sara's eyes widen. She looks scared. *Oh no.* I forgot that some people are scared of cats.

Mama has a baby picture of me sleeping next to a fluffy white cat. I was so tiny, the cat looked like it was twice my size! So when I got Pepper, I wasn't scared at all. And when Ryan came home from the hospital, I put a cat in his crib. Ryan and I have been around whiskers and claws our whole lives. Cats are as much a part of my life as Mama and Dad. When I'm scared of something, all I want to do is go home and cuddle a cat. When Pepper lies on my chest or my lap, I feel like she's lying between me and the bad stuff, protecting me. Her whiskers tickle my arm and remind me that she's going to keep me safe. How do I get Ellie, Aaliyah, and Sara to feel safe if cats are the thing they're scared of?

I think about other things that make me feel safe. Watching silly movies with my family. Snuggling in my pajamas. The smell of something baking in the oven . . .

"Sara," I say. "Can I see your list again?"

"Sure!" she says.

1. *Have a sleepover. 3. Learn how to bake a cake,* I read.

"I have an idea," I say. "A *great* one. I know how to introduce you all to my kittens. It won't be scary because we'll have cupcakes and popcorn and pajamas!"

Ellie and Aaliyah look confused.

Sara gasps in excitement. "Are you talking about . . . a *sleepover*?"

I smile. "Yes, I am. You are all officially invited to a sleepover at The Purrfect Cup."

5

The Pawjama Plan

The kittens get bigger every day. And my plan keeps growing too. It's like the jar of sourdough starter Dad keeps on the counter. Every time he adds more flour and water to it, it bubbles up and grows! And then we get to eat delicious bread. Right now, though, we're eating delicious cupcakes.

"I'm worried about Meatloaf," Ryan says. "Did you know black cats are the least likely to be adopted? People think they're creepy or something. Make sure he finds a good home, okay? He's my favorite."

Ryan blows out the seven candles he stuck on top of his cupcake.

"Seven weeks old!" he says, picking up Broccoli and holding her close to his face. Broccoli makes a little squeaky sound when Ryan picks her up. She stretches out her gray-striped legs and yawns. One of her paws taps Ryan on the nose. "And stinkier than ever."

"That's only because you forgot to give her a bath."

"You're the one who forgot!" Ryan says. "You've been too busy with your *pawjamas*."

"Pawjamas?" I laugh. "I like that."

I *have* been busy. My whole bedroom is covered in pairs of paw-printed pajamas! They're just like the ones I wore on the first day of school, except we got them on sale and they don't have names on them. Mr. Anderson gave me some old thread and a needle and showed me how to sew letters onto the pajamas. I want the pajamas to have the names of all my pawsible kitten families on them. That way, my new human friends will feel special and safe when they come over for the sleepover.

Mama said that the kittens had to be seven weeks old before meeting new humans. They needed time to be "socialized." That mostly means they've been playing with the other cats in the café a lot. Except Pepper, who still doesn't trust them. Every time I look for her, she's harder to find! Yesterday I found her under the blankets on Mama's bed. At least the kittens will play with me. Peas runs around me and pounces on my shoes.

The kittens turned seven weeks old today, and that means the big day is finally here! Tonight I host my first-ever sleepover. I've had *lots* of great ideas about what to do at the sleepover. Dad told me some of my ideas were "too much." So we won't be hiring a live band to put on a concert for the cats and the girls from school. But we *are* going to cross lots of stuff off Sara's list!

"Hey, Kira," Alex says, walking into the café. "My mom found her copy of that old movie *The Aristocats*."

"Perfect!" I say. "I can't believe I've never seen it. I love fancy cats. Thanks for finding it, Alex! You're the best."

Alex has been helping me get ready for the sleepover. We got paint from Mr. Anderson's in case Sara, Ellie, and Aaliyah want to make some cat portraits. And we popped so much popcorn I thought it was going to fill my whole kitchen!

"No problem, Kira," Alex says. "I'll always help you with your plans. How are the pajamas going?"

"I pricked my finger a lot of times doing the sewing. And my letters are a little wobbly. But I think they still turned out great!"

"Cool!" Alex pauses. She looks around the café like she doesn't know what to do next.

"I can't wait for all the *pawsible families* to get here!" I say. "I'll call you tomorrow and let you know how everything goes tonight."

"Oh, okay," Alex says. She stares at her toes. "So, uh, I guess I'll see you later?"

"Yep, see you soon!" I wave as Alex leaves the café.

Mama comes downstairs from the apartment. "Where's Alex going?" she asks. "Isn't she staying for the sleepover?"

"She was just helping me get ready," I say. "The sleepover is for pawsible kitten families. Alex can't adopt a kitten since her mom is allergic. So she would have had nothing to do."

"Did Alex say she didn't want to stay?" Mama starts. "Kira—"

Just then, the door to the café swings open again. It's Sara! And Ellie and Aaliyah are right behind her. The girls look around the café with their eyes wide. The Purrfect Cup closed a few hours ago, so it's just us and the cats. The evening light pouring in from the window is warm and golden. It makes the café look like the safest, coziest place in the world. But still, I don't want the girls to get scared by all the cats. So I bring them up to my room while Mama talks to their moms.

"Bye, Mama P!" Sara shouts as she follows me up the stairs. "See you in the morning."

Ellie plops down on the floor of my room as soon as she gets inside. Aaliyah sits in my chair by the window and crosses her legs. Sara walks around, checking out all my cat posters.

"There were *a lot* of cats downstairs," Ellie says. I can't tell if she thinks that's a good thing or a bad thing. "Can you imagine if they all got into my mom's store, Something Fishy? Cats eat fish!"

"Well, cats eat cat food made from fish. And fishy treats. But that doesn't mean they'd eat a real fish! And you could teach your kitten not to go into the fish store."

"Hmm, that's true," Ellie says.

"Where are the kittens?" Sara asks.

"I'm going to bring them in to meet you! But first, I have a special surprise."

I pull the pawjamas out of the closet and pass them out.

"These are sooo cute!" Aaliyah squeals. "Ooh, mine has letters on it. *Alooyaf.* What's that mean?"

"It's your name!" I say. "Aaliyah."

She turns the pajama shirt upside down. "Oh yeah, I see it now. Thanks, Kira!"

"Now I'll be just like Mama P and Mama J!"

Sara says. "I can't wait to show them."

We change into our pawjamas and I show the girls all my books about cats. My new friends definitely seem like they feel comfortable here. Sara really likes my book about cats in ancient Egypt.

"Mama P and I both love old things," she says. "And myths and tales and scary stories—"

Sara gets interrupted by a knock on the door. It's Ryan—and he's not alone!

"This is my little brother, Ryan," I say. "But more importantly, these are the kittens!"

Ryan holds the kittens in a basket lined with blankets. Aaliyah leans over the basket and lets out a loud, "Awww!"

Ellie looks a little scared. "Their eyes are huge!"

"They're so cute," Sara says. She looks excited and nervous. "But look at their tiny teeth! They look like mini lions. Do you think mini lions like to hunt?"

"Ryan offered to teach us all about kitten safety, so you don't have to worry about that," I say. "Well, actually, he didn't offer. I told him I'd do his chores for a week."

"*Two* weeks," Ryan reminds me. I roll my eyes.

We sit in a circle on my rug. Ellie raises her hand.

"Don't cats go to the bathroom in the house?" she asks.

"Well, humans also go to the bathroom in the house," says Ryan.

"Yeah, but people go in the toilet."

"A litter box is pretty much the same thing!" I say.

Ellie shrugs. "I guess so."

Ryan clears his throat and talks loudly. "Kitten Safety 101 starts now! First, I'm going to show you how to hold a kitten," Ryan says. "You can't just grab them around their middles, and you definitely shouldn't hold them by the back of the neck. Only their mama is supposed to do that. You should support their middle *and* hold them under their legs."

"Then they'll feel safe and you'll feel safe," I add.

Ryan gently picks up Peas.

"Cats like calm people who don't force them to do stuff. Before you pick a cat up, you should let it sniff your hand and get used to you."

Ellie reaches out her hand and lets Peas sniff her. "Her whiskers tickle," she says, laughing.

"Cats use their whiskers for lots of things, like

sensing things around them," I say. "And they use their claws to climb and hold on to stuff. Claws aren't for scratching; they're actually really important!"

"And they're sooo cute!" Aaliyah says as Ryan pulls Broccoli out of the basket. He shows her Broccoli's tiny nails and she smiles.

The other kittens look at us. They seem excited and nervous, just like their pawsible families. One by one, they crawl out of the basket.

"Oooh, a black cat! Spooky," Sara says. "They're always creeping around on Halloween."

"Meatloaf isn't spooky!" Ryan says defensively, but Sara keeps talking.

"I LOVE spooky things! Can I hold him?"

"Oh, okay, yeah! I guess he's a little spooky. In a good way."

"He would be such a good Halloween present for my parents!"

"YES!" I shout. *Oops.* I meant to say that in my head.

Ryan looks a little uncomfortable. "But you know, if you *do* take Meatloaf home, you should still bring him back here to visit. He loves it here."

"So kind of like an open adoption?" Sara says. "That's what I have! I go see my birth mom and she writes me letters. She doesn't have any cats, though. She's more of a bird person. I taught her parrot how to say my name!"

"That's cool," I say. "Sometimes I wish my cats could talk."

Aaliyah giggles. "Are you sure you want to hear what they have to say? What if they think humans smell weird?"

Just then, the door opens, but there's no one in the doorway. No one human-sized, at least.

"Pepper!" I say. "I haven't seen you in forever."

I reach out for her, but she takes one look at me surrounded by kittens and new humans—and then she bolts back out the door and down the stairs.

"Maybe I don't want to know what cats are thinking," I say. "Not all the time."

I don't think Pepper would be thinking very

nice things about me right now. I feel weird and empty. I'm so happy with the kittens and their pawsible families, but I miss Pepper. I don't understand why she won't let me hold her anymore.

"I think you scared that cat away," Sara says. "You should probably stay calm and let her come to you."

"I guess so." I scrunch up my face, trying to get rid of my sad feelings. "Um . . . does anyone want popcorn? We can watch a movie about rich fancy cats!"

"Ooooh!" Aaliyah, Sara, and Ellie exclaim together. Dad brings us big bowls of popcorn mixed with M&Ms and helps me set up the TV.

I try to fill the weird empty feeling inside me with popcorn. I'm not sure that it works, but before long, the kittens and the girls start to get comfortable with one another. Meatloaf climbs into Sara's lap to watch the movie, and Aaliyah laughs as Peas and Broccoli swat at the cats on the TV. Beans jumps onto Ellie's head and Hot Sauce snoozes on her shoulder. Ellie doesn't even seem to mind!

I don't know what's going on with Pepper, but I do know one thing *fur* sure: The Pawjama Plan was a *great idea*!

6

Ladders and Lessons

After the movie is over, Sara pulls out her list.

She crosses a bunch of things off.

Things to Do in Third Grade

1. ~~Have a sleepover.~~

2. Take Mama J to the corn maze.

3. Learn how to bake a cake.

4. Make ~~three~~ two new friends.

5. ~~Get Mama P and Daddy F the best Halloween pre-sent EVER.~~

6. Find out why ancient Romans didn't use soap.

When she crosses out number five, I can barely hold in my excitement.

"Really? You're going to give your parents Meatloaf?" I ask.

"They're going to love him!" Sara says. "But he needs a better name than Meatloaf."

"Agreed," I say. "And I think I can help you with one more thing on your list!"

"You know why the ancient Romans didn't use soap?"

"Um, no. But I can show you how to bake a

cake! My dad is an expert baker, and I'm basically as good as him."

"I love cake!" Ellie says.

"Do you have sprinkles?" Aaliyah asks.

"I always have sprinkles!" I say. Everyone follows me into our apartment kitchen, where Dad set out all the ingredients we need to make confetti cake. Ryan goes to join Mama and Dad downstairs in the café. They're deep-cleaning the café kitchen, but Dad told me to call him when we need to put the cake in the oven.

We all crowd around the mixing bowls while I show my new friends how to whisk the flour, baking soda, and salt together. Then, I show them how to crack the eggs into a separate bowl, and when I drop some eggshell in, I show them how to get the eggshell out. The cats dance around us while we bake, sniffing the bits of batter we spill on the floor. Meatloaf jumps onto a stack of pans on the counter. It makes Sara laugh.

"Hey!" she says. "Maybe I'll call him Pan. Like Peter Pan, who went to Neverland and never grew up. Or Pan the Greek god of the wild! Or Lyra's companion Pan from this book my mom told me about. He can turn into any animal he wants! Which do you think is best?"

As usual, most of the things Sara says go over my head like a cat jumping over a moon.

"I like them all!" I say.

I turn to watch as Broccoli jumps from the floor onto the counter, then onto the window ledge. She paws at the window glass. The branches of the big tree outside smack against the window, and Broccoli stares at them.

"Aww," Aaliyah says. "She wants to explore! I bet you want to go to my house, don't you, Princess?"

I smile. "Did you give Broccoli a new name?"

Aaliyah looks mischievous. "Maybe I did," she says, winking. "It's a much better name than Broccoli, don't you think?"

"WAY better," I agree.

I call for Dad, and he helps us put our cake in

the oven. Then we settle in front of the oven door to watch the cake batter bubble up into a real cake. But it takes a long time, and the kittens start to get bored.

"Should we have a dance party?" Ellie asks.

"Ooh, yes!" Aaliyah says.

"Sure!" I say. "Kittens love dancing."

We run into the living room and Sara turns on some music.

"Not too loud, or we won't hear the oven timer go off," I say. I bring out long pieces of string with feathers tied to the end. We wave them around while we dance, and the kittens chase the feathers. It looks like they're dancing too!

Just then, a song I don't know comes on. Ellie

jumps up and down. "This is my favorite song!"

She turns up the music. We dance and laugh and dance and laugh until the sides of our stomachs hurt. Finally, I collapse on the floor, exhausted. Hot Sauce pounces onto my chest.

"Hey, what's that smell?" Ellie asks.

I sit up straight. There's smoke coming into the living room from the kitchen!

"Oh no, our cake!" I say.

Sara runs downstairs to get my parents. I run into the kitchen and press the button to turn the oven off. Our cake is completely burnt! I open a window so some of the smoke can get out. I wish Alex was here. She's so good at reminding me not to forget things!

"Kira, watch out!" Ellie shouts, but it's too late. Broccoli jumps onto the window ledge—and out onto the tree outside.

"Princess!" Aaliyah cries. She leans out the window, but Broccoli climbs the branches of the tree until she's too far to reach.

Mama, Dad, and Ryan come upstairs to see what's going on.

"Goodness," Mama says.

"Goodness," Dad says.

Their faces look like they're holding in a lot more words, but I don't have time to ask them about it. We have to help Broccoli!

"What should we do?" I ask.

"We need to call my mom!" Aaliyah says.

"Is she a professional tree climber?" Ryan asks. "Please say yes."

"No, but she's a firefighter. And she's working tonight! She'll know what to do."

Mama brings us downstairs to wait while Dad airs out the kitchen. I press my cheeks against the glass windows at the front of the café, but I can't see Princess Broccoli in the tree. I hope she's okay. Maybe this whole plan was a bad idea.

Beside me, Ellie cuddles Beans in her arms and holds him tight. Sara does the same with Meatloaf. As the big red fire truck comes blaring down the street, I wish I had Pepper in my arms to keep me safe.

"Mom! You made it!" Aaliyah cries, running outside to greet the truck. Her mom has on a red firefighter uniform and a yellow hat. She looks like someone who can save Princess Broccoli. I feel a little better.

We huddle together outside while the fire-fighters pull a huge ladder off the truck.

"I can see her!" Aaliyah shouts, pointing at the tallest branches of the tree. "She's way up there. Please save her, Mom! I named her Princess."

Aaliyah's mom doesn't look scared at all. She uses the ladder to climb up and up until she reaches Princess Broccoli! Princess jumps into her arms, and they climb slowly down together.

When they reach the ground, I see the way Princess's big kitten eyes watch Aaliyah's mom. *I think she loves her.* And it looks like Aaliyah's mom feels the same.

She pulls Aaliyah in and whispers, "My sweet princesses. You're safe now."

7

Best Friends Fur-Ever

In the morning, we have confetti cake for break-fast. Not the one we made. That one was a burnt mess. But Dad made us a new one in the café kitchen.

"Well, at least I learned how *not* to bake a cake," Sara says with her mouth full of

sprinkles. She crosses that line off her list.

When the café opens, Sara, Ellie, and Aaliyah's

parents show up to bring them home. And Devin

and his mom show up too!

Devin's mom is wearing a shirt that says, *You*

can never have too many cats. She pushes past

the other parents so she can talk to Mama.

"My boy Devin says there are kittens available for adoption! We'll take three, please!"

Three?! I can't believe it!

Even Mama looks shocked. Her eyes widen, then her mouth cracks into a huge smile. "Of course!" she says. "I'll take down all your information. The kittens will be ready for adoption in about five weeks."

Aaliyah's mom asks to adopt Princess, and Ellie's mom agrees to bring Beans home as long as he doesn't eat the fish in their shop.

Sara walks up to her Mama P, holding Meatloaf. She takes a deep breath. "Mama P, this black kitten reminds me of Halloween. And I want to adopt him and bring him home. As a present for you and Dad. And all of us."

"Aw, he's so spooky and sweet," Sara's Mama P says. "This is the best present EVER! What are we going to name him?"

"I was thinking Pan," Sara says.

"Oooh, Pan like the god of the wild? Or the boy who never grew up? Or Lyra's shape-shifting companion?"

Sara smiles. "Maybe all of them. I guess we'll have to wait and see."

I count out loud. "If Devin takes three cats, and Sara, Ellie, and Aaliyah each take one cat... that's all six kittens adopted!"

Devin listens to me.

"But what will happen to the mama cat?" he asks.

"Not to worry," Mama says. "She's already spoken for."

"She *is*?" I say. I didn't even think about where Bubbles was going to live!

"As soon as your granny heard she had six kittens in a day without blinking an eye, she said she had to have her! So Granny is going to come down here soon and bring her home."

Ryan and I smile at each other. Granny is strong and fierce, just like Bubbles. They'll be the best of friends.

The Pawjama Plan was a huge success. But when I look around at all my new friends holding their new kittens, I get that weird empty feeling again. I think . . . I'm lonely. I wonder if that's how Pepper's been feeling all this time. I feel something warm brush against my leg.

"Pepper!" I say. I lean down and hold out my hand. She sniffs me, then I curl one finger under her chin to give her a little scratch. Pepper leans into my hand, then lets me pick her up. "I missed you so much," I whisper. "I'm sorry I neglected you. You're my best friend *fur-ever* and ever. How about tomorrow, we spend the whole day together? You can have unlimited treats!"

Pepper blinks three times. I think that means *yes*. I know Pepper must be the best friend ever because she loves me even though I haven't been paying her much attention.

Mama comes up beside me and sets her hand on my shoulder. Her voice is soft but serious. "Kira, we need to talk. Mrs. Patel called last night. Alex didn't say anything, but Mrs. Patel said she seemed sad. I think she feels left out."

Oh no. Have I been doing the same thing to Alex that I did to Pepper? Alex is my best human friend! Of course she must have felt left out. I was so focused on finding families for the kittens that I forgot to think about her! She even helped me with the List of Pawsibilities and the sleepover, but I didn't invite her to stay! I feel as bad as I did that time Pepper was trying to teach me how to dance and we knocked over Mama's favorite lamp. Mama forgave me. I hope Alex will too. I try to think about how I can show her that she is my very best human friend. Alex loves cats and wishes she could have one. If only there was a way to give her a whiskered best friend . . .

"Wait, Ellie!" I call out as she and her mom walk toward the door. "I have a favor to ask you."

♥ 🐾 ♥

Three hours later, I'm waiting inside The Purrfect Cup for Alex and Mrs. Patel. I can't stop tapping my foot. I hope this is a good idea. Pepper sits very still on my lap, staring at my present for Alex.

The bell dings as the front door opens and Mrs. Patel walks in, followed by Alex. I carefully put Pepper on the floor, and then jump out of my seat.

"Alex!" I say. "I'm so sorry I didn't invite you to the sleepover. I didn't know you were feeling left out and I feel so bad and I think we should have six more sleepovers that are Alex themed—"

Alex interrupts me with a big hug. Just like with Pepper, I know Alex must be the best friend ever because she forgave me before I could even finish my apology.

"Thanks, Kira," Alex says. "I'd love to have a sleepover."

"And I have something else for you!" I say. "It's not the same as a cat, exactly, but . . ."

I hold up the fish tank I got from Ellie's shop, Something Fishy.

"It's a catfish!" I say. I look at Mrs. Patel. "People with cat allergies can be around catfish. I looked it up on the internet."

Mrs. Patel smiles. Alex squeals. "*You* looked something up for *me*? Thanks, Kira! It even has whiskers like a cat! I love him! Now I just have to think of the perfect name so I can bring him to show and tell!"

The catfish is big and slimy, and I'm 99 percent sure Pepper wants to eat him. But when I look at Alex cuddling the fish tank in her arms, the empty feeling inside me melts away. I feel as full and happy as Pepper does after she's eaten a handful of treats. She jumps into my arms, and I hug her. It feels good to have my best friends back.

8

Show and Tail

The day of the pet-themed show and tell finally arrives! Mama gave Pepper a bath last night, which was not one of Mama's best ideas. Pepper hates baths almost as much as Ryan does. She jumped out of the tub and ran all over the apartment. There was slippery soap everywhere! But she sure smelled good after Mama finally got her clean. And then, after her bath, Pepper slept on my pillow. There was nowhere for me to put my head, but I didn't care. Pepper needed her beauty sleep. And now she looks amazing!

Dad holds Pepper's cat carrier for me while we walk to school. When we reach the front door, Dad leans down and says, "Good luck. Everyone's going to love you."

"Thanks, Dad," I say. He looks up at me like he just realized I was next to him! "Wait a second, were you talking to Pepper?"

"Of course not, baby girl," he says, pulling me in for a hug. "Everyone's going to love you. But, you know . . . it *is* Pepper's day."

"I know." I smile. "I'll take good care of her."

I spot Alex walking into the building. She's holding her fish tank very carefully.

"Hey, Alex!" I say. "Did you come up with a name for your fish?"

Alex has been testing out lots of different names for her fish. None of them have felt right yet. But she told me that she was determined to have a name in time for show and tell!

"Oh yes," she says. "I was up all night looking up facts about catfish. Did you know they have one hundred thousand taste buds? They really are incredible creatures. But in the end, I decided to name him Ryan."

Alex holds up the tank and looks at her catfish.

I throw my head back and laugh. "I do see the resemblance," I say. "What do you think, Pepper?"

Pepper licks her lips. Her eyes are locked on Ryan the catfish. *Uh-oh.* I think Pepper wants to eat Ryan for lunch.

Alex and I sit down in our seats. I look around

at all my classmates with their pets. Devin brought all six of his cats to school! His mom is with him. She has on a T-shirt that says *Yes! I AM the crazy cat lady!* I think she might like cats as much as me! Sara, Ellie, and Aaliyah wave when they see me. I wave back. Pan, Beans, and Princess look happy with their new owners.

"Psst, Kira." I turn around to see Jorge talking to me from three rows back. "What do you think of this doghouse? I built it myself!"

"Cool!" I say, and I mean it. Jorge's new puppy sticks its head out of the expertly engineered doghouse. Its tail wags, and its tongue hangs out of its mouth. It's a *really* cute puppy, even if it probably is smelly.

"Okay, class, we're ready to get started," Ms. Pettina says. "Let's begin with the students who have chosen to do a presentation on animals. Who wants to go first?"

No one raises their hand.

Ms. Pettina looks over all the desks. There are pets *everywhere*! I see lizards and hamsters and even a parrot!

"Hmm," Ms. Pettina says. "Did everyone bring a pet for show and tell?"

Everyone nods. I smile. My *great idea* may not have worked out *exactly* as I planned, but that doesn't mean it didn't work. All these animals found their fur-ever homes, and all my class-mates found their best friends. I feel like I could bake a six-layer cake and take a cat army to the moon! I can do anything! Then, I remember that we have a math test after show and tell. I groan. Inside her carrier, Pepper makes a grumpy face.

"Thanks for the sympathy," I say. At least I have my two best friends by my side. With them, I'm ready for whatever comes next. Even if it's math.

♥ 🐾 ♥

The day after show and tell, I get ready to host my second-ever sleepover. This time I've got my best friend, Pepper, to help me set up. We're making sure *all* the windows are locked. I can't wait for Alex, Sara, Ellie, and Aaliyah to come over.

I find Ryan sitting at the kitchen table. His face reminds me of Pepper's grumpy cat face.

"Ugh, it smells gross in here! Ryan, what are you eating?"

I look down at the plate in front of him. It's piled with meatloaf, beans, broccoli, peas, and tuna. There's a big bottle of hot sauce next to the plate.

Ryan stuffs a big forkful of tuna and broccoli in his mouth. He grimaces. "I'm eating my least favorite foods."

"Uh, that sounds like a bad idea! Worse than that time I tried to make healthy cookies. I wanted to convince Dad that we should be allowed to eat dessert for dinner."

Ryan shakes hot sauce onto his peas. He sighs, and his voice becomes small. "I thought naming the kittens after my least favorite foods would make it easier to say goodbye to them when they got adopted. I'm eating my least favorite foods to remind myself how bad they are and how much I don't miss having Meatloaf around."

Oh no. Poor Ryan. I sit down and put my arm around his shoulder. "Is it working?"

He shakes his head. "No. I love Meatloaf."

He puts a piece of meatloaf in his mouth and shudders.

"I love Meatloaf too. Can I have a piece?"

He looks grateful. "If you really want some."

I fit the rest of the meatloaf on my fork so Ryan doesn't have to eat any more. Then I pull out Mama's laptop.

"Maybe Sara will bring Pan—I mean, Meatloaf, over tonight. It's an open adoption, remember? And even if she doesn't, Sara's mom has been posting videos of them all day. Want to watch?"

Ryan nods. We take turns eating Ryan's least favorite foods while we watch videos of Sara playing with Pan. She and Pan race down their hallway, pretending that they are traveling between Mount Olympus and Earth at the speed of light. Then Sara pretends that Pan has transformed into a tiger. She and her mom giggle as he pounces on his feather cat toy. In the last video, Sara picks Pan up and cuddles him in her arms and shouts that they will never grow up. I know that one day Pan will turn from a kitten into a cat and Sara will become an adult, but that day feels a long ways away. I'd rather think about Neverland and kittens.

When the plate of terrible foods is empty, my stomach hurts but my heart feels happy. I look over at Ryan and he smiles.

"That was a good idea," he says.

I smile back. "I know."

Turn the page for a sneak peek at

Kira's next *great idea* in . . .

Kitten Around

"While we're gone, Granny will be in charge," Mama says.

I frown. Granny is our *granny*, so of course she's in charge. I know that. But I don't know why Mama doesn't want me to be the leader. After all, I know a lot about running the café and I *definitely* know more about cats. I've lived here my whole life!

Dad nods, agreeing with Mama. "Remember to listen to your grandma and help her out as much as you can. And listen to each other, too—that's just as important. Otherwise your mama and I will never leave you alone again. Not even when you turn eighteen."

Mama and Dad do one more walk-through

of the café, then give us another hug before leaving. The bell rings as the door to the café opens and shuts. Granny locks it behind them. Mama and Dad are gone.

Granny sighs, then turns around and winks at me. "What's that you were saying about *great ideas* earlier? This café could use a little pick-me-up."

My mouth drops open in excitement. Granny still wants me to use my ideas! Maybe this is how I'll show Mama that I know how to run a café just like she does. I'll *jam-pack* this weekend with a whole bunch of ideas. Dad told me about jam-packing things. It means that you stuff a lot of things into one space, like when you boil a big pot of strawberries and sugar together until they become sweet, simmering jam and then you pack the jam into a jar. Or like when you stuff so much strawberry jam on your peanut-butter-and-jelly sandwich that the bread soaks through and turns pink. That's what I'm going to do. I'm going to stuff so many of my ideas into this weekend that it becomes Kira-colored. When Mama comes home, she'll see how awesome all of my ideas are! Then she'll know that I can help her with more than making the bed.

I can't wait!